KAPOC, THE KILLER CROC

STORY BY
MARCIA VAUGHAN

PICTURES BY
EUGENIE FERNANDES

Silver Burdett Press

For Dick and Barbara Powell
with lots of love—*M.V.*

For Matthew—*E.F.*

Published by Silver Burdett Press, a division of Paramount Publishing,
250 James Street, Morristown, New Jersey 07960.
Manufactured in the United States of America.
10 9 8 7 6 5 4 3 2 1
Library of Congress Cataloging-in-Publication Data
Vaughan, Marcia K.
Kapoc, the killer croc / by Marcia Vaughan; illustrated by Eugenie Fernandes.
p.   cm.—(Animal fair series)
Summary: A crocodile and a sloth have a life-or-death race on the Amazon.
ISBN 0-382-24075-8 (HC).—ISBN 0-382-24069-3 (LSB).—
ISBN 0-382-24602-0 (SC)
[1. Crocodiles—Fiction.   2. Sloths—Fiction.   3. Jungle Animals—Fiction.]
I. Fernandes, Eugenie, ill.   II. Title.   III. Series: Vaughan, Marcia K.   Animal
fair series.
PZ7.V452Kap 1994   [E]—dc20   91-35224   CIP   AC

Kapoc is a Caiman, a member of the Crocodilian family.

One misty morning in the rain forest, Toucan, Spider Monkey, and Sloth gathered at the edge of the river when something strange came drifting towards them.

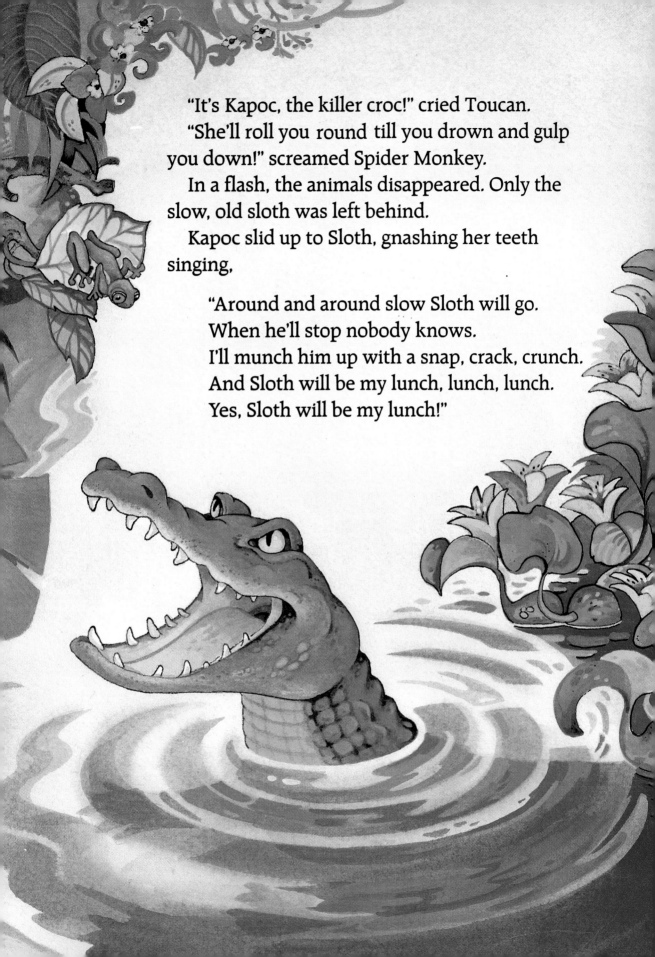

"It's Kapoc, the killer croc!" cried Toucan.

"She'll roll you round till you drown and gulp you down!" screamed Spider Monkey.

In a flash, the animals disappeared. Only the slow, old sloth was left behind.

Kapoc slid up to Sloth, gnashing her teeth singing,

"Around and around slow Sloth will go.
When he'll stop nobody knows.
I'll munch him up with a snap, crack, crunch.
And Sloth will be my lunch, lunch, lunch.
Yes, Sloth will be my lunch!"

"You can't catch me," said Sloth slowly.
"Of course I can. I'm by far the fastest animal in the rain forest," bragged Kapoc. "You, Sloth, are by far the slowest."

"Me slow?" yawned Sloth. "Only on the ground am I as slow as a snail. But I can race across the roof of the rain forest faster than you can swim down the Amazon River."

Kapoc was furious. "A whole family of sloths could never beat me!" she said, snapping her jaws.

"Yes, I can," declared Sloth.

"Then prove it. Race me right now," Kapoc hissed.

"I'd like to race you now, but I need my nap," Sloth replied. "Wait till tomorrow at sunrise, and I will be as fast as lightning. Then I'll race you all the way to the great waterfall."

"And if I win," grinned Kapoc, smacking her tail on the mud, "you must promise to be my lunch."

"And if I win," Sloth agreed, "you must promise *never* to eat another animal from this rain forest."

"I promise," nodded Kapoc, crossing her toes. "I'll see you at sunrise." She slid down the muddy bank into the river and disappeared.

So Toucan told Tapir…Tapir told Boa
Constrictor…Boa Constrictor told Spider
Monkey…and Spider Monkey told Parrot.
By moonrise, the whole rain forest was abuzz
with the news of the great race.

That night, while Kapoc snored, Sloth, his wife, children, aunts, uncles, and cousins were busy whispering a secret through the treetops.

"Are you ready?" Kapoc called the next morning.

"Yes, I am," Sloth answered in a high, sweet voice.

"Why do you sound so strange today?" snapped Kapoc.

"Last night I was bitten by a boolie bug and my throat is sore."

Kapoc's eyes flashed. "If you're too sick to race, you can come right down and be my breakfast."

"Sick or not, I can still beat you to the waterfall," Sloth answered.

As the sun splashed its first red rays across the sky, the race began.

With a grim grin, Kapoc slid into the water and drifted lazily down the river, her tail swaying slowly from side to side as she sang,

"Around and around slow Sloth will go.
When he'll stop nobody knows.
I'll munch him up with a snap, crack, crunch.
And Sloth will be my lunch, lunch, lunch.
Yes, Sloth will be my lunch."

At the first bend, Kapoc stopped and looked
up into the trees, calling,

"Sloth, Sloth, hello, halloo.
Sloth, Sloth, where are you?"

Up popped Sloth.

"Here I am, but not for long.
If you think you can beat me, Kapoc,
you're wrong."

So Kapoc swam a little faster down the river.
At the second bend, she stopped and called,

"Sloth, Sloth, hello, halloo.
Sloth, Sloth, where are you?"

And Sloth answered,

"Here I am, but not for long.
If you think you can beat me, Kapoc,
you're wrong."

So Kapoc swam even faster.
At the third bend, Kapoc called again. And
again Sloth sang out,

"Here I am, but not for long.
  If you think you can beat me, Kapoc,
you're wrong."

  With a snort, Kapoc charged down the river,
her tail lashing madly from side to side. Yet no
matter how swiftly she swam, Kapoc could not
overtake Sloth. At every turn in the river she
called to Sloth, who answered,

  "Here I am, but not for long.
  If you think you can beat me, Kapoc,
  you're *wrong*."

In a rage, Kapoc raced down the rapids. Splashing and thrashing and gnashing, she sped round bend after bend, until all of a sudden, she heard the river roaring as it thundered over the edge of the great waterfall.

"I'm going to win," cried Kapoc. "No sloth can ever beat me now. And all this racing has made me hungry.

"Around and around slow Sloth will go.
When he'll stop nobody knows.
I'll munch him up with a snap, crack, crunch.
And Sloth will be my lunch, lunch, lunch.
Yes, Sloth will be my... *what*!"

Kapoc could not finish her song. For right ahead of her, moving as slowly as a snail toward the finish line, was Sloth!

There was no stopping Kapoc now. With one last thrash of her mighty tail, that crocodile swam faster and faster and faster and *faster*.

"I win. I win!" cried Kapoc, rocketing down the river, flying across the finish line, and shooting straight out over the edge of the waterfall like a spear!

Then Sloth, who had been waiting at the
finish line all along, called,

"Bally bally bally hoo.
It's safe to come out, all of you."

Hearing this, Sloth's wife and all of his
family peeked out from their hiding places
in the treetops.

As Kapoc went spinning out of sight, Sloth
and all the animals in the rain forest sang,

"Around and around old Kapoc goes.
When she'll stop nobody knows.
She'll hit the rocks with a snap, crack, crunch.
And we won't be her lunch, lunch, lunch.
No, we won't be her lunch!"